(8)

CASEBUSTERS

Catch a Crooked Clown

Disney *Adventures*

⑧

CASEBUSTERS

Catch a Crooked Clown

By Joan Lowery Nixon

DISNEY PRESS

114 Fifth Avenue
New York, NY 10011-5690

With love to my granddaughter Kathryn Joan McGowan—J. L. N.

Printed in the United States of America.

First Edition
1 3 5 7 9 10 8 6 4 2

Library of Congress Catalog Card Number: 96-84827
ISBN: 0-7868-4081-1 (pbk.)

1

BRIAN PULLED HIS bike to a quick stop
as he saw a crowd gathering up ahead.
"What's going on?" Sean yelled. He
stopped his bike next to Brian's and hopped off.

"There's one way to find out," Brian said,
"but we'll have to make it fast. It's got to be at
least four o'clock, and we're supposed to be
home by five." He leaned his bike into a nearby
rack and ran down the sidewalk to join the
crowd, which was opposite the open main
doors of a small shopping mall. Sean was right
behind him.

Stumbling in his very large shoes, a clown in a wild green wig and a baggy costume pushed through the crowd. His painted grin and black crisscross eyes made him look as though he'd burst out laughing at any minute. Flip-flopping along, he handed out balloons and flyers.

Brian reached for a flyer and read it. "Hey Sean," he said, "the Star-Spangled Circus will have its grand-opening performance tomorrow evening. Want to go?"

"Sure," Sean said, but his attention was on the small monkey that rode on the clown's left shoulder. The monkey wore a loose leather collar that was attached to a short leash, and the monkey kept jerking at the collar, as though he were unhappy about being tied up.

"Oh-oh," Sean said. "Bri, do you know what I think? That collar—"

Suddenly, the monkey pulled the collar over

his head, leaped from the clown's shoulder, and dashed through the nearby open door to the mall.

"That's just what I thought he'd do," Sean yelled.

Some of the onlookers shrieked, and some of them laughed. Almost all of them ran with the stumbling, tripping clown after the monkey. Brian and Sean hurried after them.

The nearest store was Hart's Jewels. The monkey, with the clown right behind him, jumped from counter to counter, then out the entrance and into the gift shop next door.

If I can just get ahead of him, Sean thought. The monkey leaped, and Sean grabbed for him, but missed.

"Darn!" Sean said and tried again, but this time the monkey dove right over Sean's head.

From there the monkey raced into a sportswear store. The clown and the yelling, laughing crowd gave chase.

It was just a hop and a swing into the next store—a small drugstore. The monkey would have made it except for Sean, who saw where he'd be heading and waited for him at the door. The monkey leaped, and Sean caught him, holding him tightly.

"There, there," Sean murmured, as the monkey huddled against him, trembling. "You're okay, little guy. Don't be afraid."

Brian and the drugstore owner kept the crowd back until the clown caught up.

"Your monkey's collar is too loose." Sean said to the clown. "He was able to pull it right over his head."

The clown didn't speak. His real lips, inside the painted grin, looked tight and angry, and he glared at Sean. He fastened the collar on the monkey, snatched him out of Sean's arms, and stumbled and tripped his way out of the mall and to the sidewalk.

With the excitement over, the onlookers walked away. But Brian and Sean followed the clown. They watched him step into a dark brown sedan. They weren't able to see the driver through the tinted windows, but Brian pulled out his private investigator's notebook and pen and jotted down the license plate as the car drove off in the direction of the circus grounds.

"Why do you want his license number?" Sean asked. "You know the clown's with the circus."

"Private investigators never take anything for granted," Brian told him.

Sean shrugged. "Maybe you're right. Maybe that clown isn't with the circus. Circus clowns are supposed to be funny, but this one was a real grouch." He thought a moment, then said, "It sounds weird, Bri, and don't laugh. But I think that clown was mad at me for saying that the monkey's collar was too loose. It was kinda like he knew it was loose on purpose, but he didn't want anyone else to know."

Brian didn't laugh. He said, "The clown should have thanked you for catching his monkey, but he didn't. He didn't say anything to you at all."

Sean shrugged. "Okay, so he was rude. It doesn't matter, does it?"

"I don't know," Brian said. "Maybe we should find out."

2

DURING THE REST of the day Sean worked so hard studying for a history test, he forgot all about the clown. So he was surprised when a friend of the family, Detective Sergeant Thomas Kerry, came to the Quinns' home that evening to talk to Brian and Sean.

"Gus Hart told me you were in the crowd that chased after the monkey this afternoon," he said.

Mrs. Quinn's eyebrows shot up. "What monkey?" she asked.

"What's this about a monkey?" Mr. Quinn

asked at the same time.

"Brian, suppose you tell your parents what happened. Sean can fill in," Sergeant Kerry said. "Describe everything you saw. I'd like to hear all the details."

Brian nodded. "There was a clown walking along Main Street. He handed out flyers about the opening performance of the Star-Spangled Circus tomorrow night. He was about five ten or eleven, and he was wearing huge shoes he could hardly walk in, baggy clothes, a straw hat with a daisy on it, and a big grin."

"And he was real crabby," Sean said.

Sergeant Kerry stopped writing. "I thought Brian said he was grinning."

"The grin was painted on," Sean said. "Besides, he didn't even thank me."

"Thank you? For what?" Mrs. Quinn asked.

"Because I caught his monkey," Sean said.

Mr. Quinn gave a long sigh. "What are we talking about?" he asked.

Sergeant Kerry broke in. "Suppose we let Brian finish telling what happened. Then Sean can add his comments."

Brian went on to describe the chase. "Sean figured out where the monkey would run next, so he was waiting for him outside the drugstore and—"

"I caught him!" Sean interrupted. "All by myself!"

"Good for you, dear." Mrs. Quinn smiled at Sean.

Brian looked at Sergeant Kerry. "What else happened? Something did, or you wouldn't be here."

"I'm here because of a complaint," Sergeant Kerry said. "The owners of three of the shops in that mall claim they were burglarized. Gus

Hart, in the jewelry shop; Merilee Hughes, in the gift shop; and Ron Harris in the sportswear shop. They all noticed during the late afternoon that small items were missing from their stores. They can't be positive—especially Hart, who was at home working on his expenses at the time—but they think the thefts happened while the clown was rushing through the aisles, trying to catch the monkey."

"There were lots of people there besides the clown," Brian said. "I think everyone who'd been watching the clown ran into the mall after the monkey."

Sergeant Kerry nodded. "Just between us, Gus Hart complains every time carnivals or circuses come to town. He insists they're bad for business because people spend money with them, instead of with the stores in Redoaks." He shrugged. "However, he claims that a gold bracelet and necklace were stolen from a display case on the counter, so I have to investigate the burglary."

He looked at his notebook again, then back to Brian. "Do you have any idea what time the monkey chase took place? The clerks in the shops can't agree."

"The clock over Mr. Hart's desk was at 4:02 P.M.," Brian said. "It's a large clock, and I noticed it."

"And remembered the time. You're a good investigator," Mr. Quinn said proudly.

"Did you notice any suspicious actions on the part of the clown or any of the others who ran into the store?" Sergeant Kerry asked.

Brian and Sean looked at each other, then shook their heads.

"I was paying more attention to the monkey than to the people," Brian said.

"Me, too," Sean said. "I was thinking of how scared the poor monkey looked and how I could catch him."

Brian pulled out his notebook, found the page he wanted, and handed it to Sergeant Kerry. "Someone in a brown sedan with tinted windows picked up the clown. I copied the license plate."

"Very good," Sergeant Kerry said. He wrote down the information. Then he opened his briefcase and took out a sketch of a clown face. "Do you recognize this?" he asked.

"Yes," Brian and Sean answered at the same time.

"That's him," Brian said. "How'd you find a witness who could remember everything about the face so clearly?"

"The sketch isn't from a witness description," Sergeant Kerry said. "It's from one of the circus ads. Crackers the Clown. His real name is Marco Moroney. He comes from a long line of circus clowns. He and his partner, Dale Erhard, own the Star-Spangled Circus together."

Mr. Quinn broke in. "Does this Marco Moroney have a list of prior arrests? Has he pulled this trick in other towns in which the circus has appeared?"

Sergeant Kerry shook his head. "No. That's what's strange about this situation. Moroney doesn't have a police record, and there's never been a single complaint from local merchants when the Star-Spangled Circus was around." He glanced again at the picture before he tucked it away. "However, a number of people—like you two—identified this picture right away."

Sergeant Kerry thanked Brian and Sean for

their help. Then he got to his feet and headed to the door. Mr. Quinn, who walked with him, asked, "What's your next step, Tom?"

"One of my assistants is getting a search warrant, and we're going to the circus grounds to look for the stolen items and talk to Moroney," Sergeant Kerry said.

Sean thought about the clown's angry glare. Sergeant Kerry would find out that Marco Moroney wasn't as friendly as his makeup made him appear to be. He was downright mean!

3

THE NEXT DAY Brian and Sean met on their way home from school. They bent over the handlebars of their bikes and raced each other the rest of the way. But as they turned into the driveway next to their house, they came to a skidding stop.

A sad-looking boy, about Sean's size, was sitting on the steps to their front porch, his bike lying on the grass near his feet. He glanced up at them, scrambled to his feet, and rubbed his reddened eyes. "Are you the Casebusters?" he called.

Brian and Sean laid their bikes on the grass

and walked to the porch. "Yes, we're the Casebusters. I'm Brian and this is Sean," Brian answered.

"I'm Dan Moroney," the boy said.

"Moroney?" Sean repeated. "Oh, but Moroney is . . ."

Dan interrupted. "That's right. My dad's Crackers the Clown. It's his picture the police have—the picture a lot of people identified yesterday. But my dad didn't steal anything. He wasn't even in town yesterday. He's half owner of the circus, and he was busy helping to set up the tents. People who identified that drawing think my dad's guilty, but he isn't!"

Brian sat on the steps. Sean and Dan sat with him. "Last night Detective Tom Kerry went to see your dad, didn't he?" Brian asked. He wondered if Dan's father had been arrested.

"He was there on the circus grounds," Dan

said. "Some policemen came with him, and they looked for whatever stuff was stolen, but they didn't find anything."

Brian kept on. "Where's your dad now?"

"They didn't arrest him, if that's what you mean," Dan said, "but I'm worried that sooner or later they'll decide that Dad was the only one who could have done it, and *then* they'll arrest him."

Sean broke in. "If your dad was working to help set up the tents, he'd have an alibi, wouldn't he? Some of the people there would have seen him."

"Just for part of the time, because he also was working alone in the office in our trailer," Dan said. "And none of the people who saw him during the afternoon knew what time it was. Either they weren't wearing watches or they weren't paying attention to the time."

Dan's voice came out like a sob. "They weren't any help at all."

"Hey, it's going to be okay," Sean said. "The Casebusters usually solve their cases."

Dan looked up eagerly. "That's what Sergeant Kerry said. I told him that my dad and I don't have much money, so we couldn't hire a private investigator to help us. That's when he told me about you guys. He said we could afford you."

"Because we're free," Sean said.

"We'll take the case," Brian said. He got right down to business, pulling out his notebook and pen. He made a few notations, then asked, "Dan, do you think that the thief was another clown who paints his face exactly like your father's clown face?"

"No," Dan answered. "Every clown's face is registered. No two clowns look alike. It had to be someone dressed in my dad's costume who knew exactly how he puts on his clown face so he could copy it."

"That means it would have to be someone in the circus," Sean said.

Dan shook his head. "It could be someone outside the circus. Crackers the Clown's face has been in newspapers and magazines—once even in a TV commercial."

"How about the rest of his costume?" Brian asked. "Is it kept in a special place, or is it where other people can get to it?"

"Whenever we get to a new town, all the costumes are cleaned and hung up in the costume tent, where the performers have room to change," Dan said.

"We're going to have to see this tent. We'll need to visit the circus lot," Brian said.

"No problem," Dan said. He stood up. "Let's go."

But Brian held up a hand. "Sean, write a note for Mom and stick it on the refrigerator. Tell her where we'll be."

As Sean stood up, picking up his backpack, Brian said, "Take my books inside, too. Okay?"

"Sean, do this. Sean, do that," Sean answered. "Who'd you boss around last year?"

"You," Brian said. He broke into a grin. "Okay, I'll do it myself. I want to ask Dan one question first."

Brian turned to Dan. "The person who's trying to look just like your dad might be trying to set him up. Does your dad have any enemies?"

Dan looked uncomfortable. "Enemies? Dad's a real nice guy. Everybody likes him."

"You didn't answer my question," Brian said.

Dan picked up his bike and straddled it. "If

you want to see the circus lot before dark, we'd better get going. Hurry up."

Brian didn't ask his question again. There'd be time for that later. I wonder, he thought, is Dan hiding some information we ought to know? And if he is . . . Why?

THE CIRCUS LOT was busy with people putting the finishing touches on the food stands and the carnival games. A pair of elephants was being washed with long-handled brushes, and everyone who passed Brian, Sean, and Dan seemed to be in a hurry.

Some of them waved at Dan and smiled, but no one asked what Brian and Sean were doing there. No one seemed to care. Brian stopped to write in his notebook: *Poor security.*

At one side of the lot were a row of trailers, trucks, and a few cars. Brian spotted the brown sedan like the one he'd seen at the mall.

"Whose car is that brown one?" he asked Dan.

"Oh, those cars and trucks and stuff are all property of the circus," Dan said.

"Who drives the brown sedan?"

Dan shrugged. "Sometimes Dad, sometimes his partner." He lifted a flap in the costume tent and ducked inside. Brian and Sean followed. Opposite them was another flap in the canvas, this one pinned open.

From the activity taking place beyond, Brian could see that the opening led directly inside the main tent. Dan had said that some of the performers went directly from the costume tent into the main tent.

Brian looked around at the racks of glittery, colorful costumes, which lined one side of the tent. "No one asked what we were doing here," he said to Dan. "Was that because we were with you?"

Dan looked surprised. "I don't know. I don't think so."

"I mean, anyone—circus people or outsiders—could easily sneak into the tent and help themselves to a costume, couldn't they?" Brian asked.

Dan thought a moment. "I suppose so," he said, "but it would be kind of weird. No one's ever done it before."

Sean examined the row of tables and mirrors, surrounded by lights. He picked up a long, blond wig on a Styrofoam stand. "Who wears this?" he asked.

"Phoebe, who rides on one of the elephants," Dan said. "You better put it down. If Phoebe thinks you touched it, she'll have a screaming fit."

Sean pointed to another wig stand. "What's this? It looks like a big green mop."

Dan laughed. "It's my dad's clown wig."

Brian perched on a canvas folding chair, and Sean came over to join him. "Sit down, Dan," Brian said. "Sean and I have to learn a lot more before we can do any more work on your case."

Dan squirmed on his chair before he said, "Like what?"

"Like the question you wouldn't answer," Brian said. "So I'll ask it again. Does your dad have any enemies?"

"Not exactly," Dan said.

"What does 'not exactly' mean?" Sean asked.

Dan hesitated. "There's something I kind of found out by accident, but I'm not supposed to talk about it."

Brian made his voice sound very official.

"Anything you say to the Casebusters is confidential," he said.

"That means we won't talk about it to anybody," Sean said. "We promise."

"And what you tell us may help us solve the case and prove your father is innocent," Brian added.

Dan thought a moment. Then he said, "Okay. When I said 'not exactly,' I meant that Dad is having problems with some people, but they're not really enemies. Like his partner Dale Erhard. He's the lion tamer and ringmaster, and he keeps the books, too. I overheard him telling Dad that the circus isn't making a big enough profit for two partners. He wants Dad to sell out to him."

"How does your Dad feel about this?" Sean asked.

"He doesn't even want to think about it," Dan answered. "The circus has been in Dad's family for three generations, and he's not about to sell out."

Brian wrote down everything Dan had said. Then he looked up. "Does your dad have problems with anybody else?"

"Yeah," Dan said. "With Laura Lee and Ray Spangler. They're the trapeze artists. They have a contract with Dad that runs for another four or five years. I forget which. They want to break the contract and accept an offer they got from a large circus company in France. But Dad needs them and doesn't want to let them go right now while the circus is having financial trouble. They're really good, and they draw a lot of customers."

Dan thought a minute, then sighed. "Maybe I shouldn't say anything about Eric Lewis. He hasn't really done anything, but he *is* kind of a problem."

"Who's Eric Lewis?" Sean asked.

"He's this nineteen-year-old guy who's been in trouble with the police a couple of times, so he's on probation. Dad rescued Eric by taking him in and giving him a job. Dad called it a second chance for the right kind of life. Dad says if Eric works steady and stays out of trouble, he'll be okay."

"He's lucky that your father wants to help him," Brian said.

Dan shrugged. "Eric doesn't think so. He gets mad real easy at practically anything and hides out sometimes, instead of doing his work. If Dad tries to talk to him, he says he doesn't want any lectures."

"How did Eric get into trouble with the police?" Sean asked.

"Shoplifting," Dan said.

Brian and Sean looked at each other.

"That's what the clown was accused of doing," Brian said.

"Eric could have dressed up in the clown costume," Sean said.

Dan shook his head. "Eric might steal, but I don't think he'd make it look like Dad did it. He owes a lot to Dad."

Brian began to close his notebook, but Dan said, "There is someone else who's been giving Dad trouble. That guy from the jewelry store has been hanging around the lot, last night and today. He pokes around and glares at people."

"Gus Hart," Sean said.

"Yeah, that's him."

"But his shop was one that was burglarized," Sean said. "He would have had to commit the burglary himself."

"Mr. Hart wants to keep circuses and carnivals out of Redoaks," Brian said. "He might have thought that scaring people with a burglary and blaming it on someone in the circus would be a way to do it."

Brian looked at his watch. "It's getting late, Dan. We'll have to go in a few minutes. Can we get a look at the people you told us about?"

"The Spanglers and Dale Erhard will be in the show tonight. Are you coming?"

Sean nodded. "Yeah. Mom and Dad are taking us."

But Brian said, "I'd like to get a good look at them ahead of time. Eric Lewis, too."

"Okay," Dan said. "Come on. I'll point them out." He led them through the flap to the main tent.

"Stay right here," Brian said. " I don't want them to notice us."

The Spanglers were rehearsing on the high trapeze, and Dale Erhard was in the center ring, setting things up. Luckily, they were all too busy to pay attention to Brian and Sean.

"There are three of our suspects," Sean said, "and we know what Gus Hart looks like. Can we get a good look at the other suspect—Eric Lewis?"

Someone pushed through the entrance to the costume tent. Brian was shoved aside so roughly he tripped, falling into Sean and Dan. The three of them landed on the ground in a heap.

A stocky young man, dressed in a dirty T-shirt and jeans, leaned over them, scowling. "What are you kids doing, snooping around here? You don't belong on the circus property. Pick yourselves up, and get out of here!"

"It's okay. They're with me," Dan said.

"Yeah? Well, you're a snoop, too," the man snapped, "and if you kids don't watch out, your snooping's going to get you into real trouble."

He stomped back into the costume tent and was gone.

"Wow! That guy is scary!" Sean said. "Who *was* that?"

"That was Eric Lewis." Dan gulped. "And I bet he heard everything we were talking about!"

5

NIGHTTIME AT the circus was spectacular, with strings of brightly colored lights outlining the booths and tents. The long beams from klieg lights swept the sky, and vendors with bags of popcorn and peanuts worked their way through the crowds hurrying into the main tent to see the show.

Dan had been watching for Brian and Sean, and he ran to meet them.

As he was introduced to the Quinns, Mr. Quinn said, "You have a large audience tonight, Dan."

"We almost always get large audiences," Dan said. "Lots of times the seats are sold out for every performance. People love circuses."

Sean groaned as he saw Debbie Jean Parker with her parents, and he ducked behind Brian before she spotted him.

"Could I take Brian and Sean backstage for a few minutes?" Dan asked.

"Of course," Mrs. Quinn said. She handed Brian two tickets. "These will get you inside. We'll meet you at our seats."

"Hey, Sean!" Debbie Jean yelled. She jumped up and down and waved at Sean.

"Let's go!" Sean said. "Quick!"

"Who was that?" Dan asked as they hurried back to the costume tent.

"A girl in Sean's fourth-grade class," Brian answered. "I think she kinda likes him."

Sean groaned and made a face. "Debbie

Jean drives me crazy!" he said.

Dan looked sympathetic. "Well forget her. Come and meet my dad. I want you to see what a nice guy he is. And I'd like him to meet *you*."

He led Brian and Sean into the costume tent, which was filled with performers who were giving last-minute touches to their costumes and makeup. Marco Moroney was seated before one of the mirrors, putting on his clown wig.

"Dad," Dan said, "I want you to meet Brian and Sean Quinn."

Mr. Moroney's eyes twinkled, and he grinned inside his broad, red clown grin. "Hello, hello, hello," he said. As Mr. Moroney shook Sean's hand, his fat clown fingers seemed to wiggle in every direction.

Sean laughed. Mr. Moroney seemed like a friendly guy, and Sean liked him immediately.

"You're two fine-looking young men," Mr. Moroney said to Brian and Sean. "Have you ever thought of working some day with a circus?"

"It sounds like fun," Brian said politely and smiled.

"Bri can't be a circus performer," Sean said. "He's already got a job. He's a private investigator."

Brian gave Sean a warning look. "Sean," he said.

In his excitement, Dan blurted out, "Sean's an investigator, too. Brian and Sean are the Casebusters, and they've solved lots of crimes. That's why I hired them to investigate and find out who the fake clown is—the one who's pretending to be you!"

For a moment there was silence in the tent. Brian glanced around to see Dale Erhard and Laura Lee and Ray Spangler staring at him.

Then everyone looked away and began talking at once.

Mr. Moroney's forehead puckered as he thought. "Isn't that a little risky, being investigators at your ages?" he asked.

"Our dad's a private investigator," Sean answered. "He's taught us to be careful."

"And are you?"

Sean looked at Brian. "Ummm, most of the time," Sean said.

"We'd better find our seats," Brian said quickly. "We're glad to meet you, Mr. Moroney. See you later, Dan."

As he pushed Sean out of the costume tent, Brian complained, "You and Dan blew our cover. Now all the suspects know what we're doing."

"Does it make any difference?" Sean asked. "Eric already found out. He probably told them."

Brian remembered the surprised looks on the faces of the Spanglers, the wary glance of Dale Erhard. "I don't think so," he said.

As they joined the line to enter the main tent, Brian pulled out the tickets Mrs. Quinn had given them. "Sean," he said, "while we're on the circus lot, we'll have to be extra watchful and careful."

But Sean was already scrambling over the seats to reach their parents.

A trumpet sounded just outside the main entrance to the tent, and a band began marching in, leading the performers' parade. Brian hurried to join the rest of his family.

The show was terrific. The clowns made everyone laugh. The Spanglers swung and somersaulted in the light of the spotlights that swept back and forth across the top of the tent. Their trapeze act was so exciting that at times people gasped and shrieked. The horses and elephants performed their tricks perfectly, and the act with the trained lions brought the audience to its feet. Mr. Erhard stood in the spotlight and bowed again and again.

Intermission was announced, and Sean plopped down onto his seat in the bleachers, almost landing on Debbie Jean.

"I couldn't stand it when the trainer put his head in the lion's mouth!" she shouted.

Sean rubbed his ear. "Your mother's calling you," he said.

"No, she's not," Debbie Jean said. "Our seats are just two rows behind yours, and Mom told me I could climb down here and say hello to you."

"You better climb back, because I can't talk to you. I'm on a case," Sean said.

Debbie Jean rolled her eyes. "Oh, come on.

You're on a case in the circus? I don't believe that."

She started to say something else, then stopped, her mouth still open. She recovered and said, "Wait a minute. That clown who stole things . . . That's your case, isn't it?"

"Shhhh!" Sean said. "We don't want everybody here to know about it."

"Are you looking for clues?" Debbie Jean asked. "I can do that. I want to help. I bet I can solve the case before you do."

One of the circus employees reached up and handed Brian a folded note. The man disappeared under the bleachers before either Brian or Sean was able to get a good look at him.

"What's that?" Sean asked as Brian read the note.

"It's from Dan," Brian said. "He wants to

meet with us right away. He has some new information."

Debbie Jean was leaning over Sean's shoulder to listen.

"Let's go," Sean whispered to Brian. Sean turned to Mrs. Quinn and said, "We'll be right back, Mom." Before she could answer, he squeezed through the people on the bleachers until he reached the ground.

Brian hurried down behind him, and they left the tent through the main opening.

"Where does Dan want us to meet him?" Sean asked.

"Behind the lion cages, where no one will hear us," Brian answered.

They passed the elephants and a group of horses decorated with plumes and spangles. There were plenty of people getting these animals ready to perform again. But back behind the lion cages, it was dark and quiet.

One of the lions snuffled, and Sean shuddered. As his eyes grew used to the darkness he could see the lion prowling up and down in his cage. He seemed to be staring right at Sean.

"Where is Dan, anyway?" Sean asked. "How long do we have to wait for him?"

The lion snuffled again. This time Brian jumped. "Maybe we should look for Dan," he said.

As Brian took a step forward, so did the lion, pressing his nose against the bars of his cage.

To Brian's and Sean's horror, the door of the cage swung open, and the lion leaped out. It stood motionless, staring at them eye to eye.

6

SEAN AND BRIAN frantically yelled for help and made a dash for the top of the nearest cage. The lion under them snarled and scratched at its bars, but Sean and Brian kept their eyes on the lion that was loose. Lions could jump. They'd seen this one do it during the lion show. What if he decided to jump on top of the cage to get them?

"Help!" Sean shouted again.

"Quiet!" a firm voice below them said.

Brian and Sean looked down to see Dale Erhard, the ringmaster. He cracked a whip, making loud snapping noises as he slowly walked toward the lion.

The lion began to back up, whirled around, and jumped into his cage. Mr. Erhard snapped the padlock shut, then tuned to look up at Brian and Sean. His face was red with anger.

"Get down from there!" he ordered. He distracted the lion inside the cage while Brian and Sean scrambled to the ground, moving well out of reach of any of the caged animals.

Other circus employees had gathered; among them were Dan, Mr. Moroney, and Eric. Dan looked frightened and Mr. Moroney, worried, but Eric just scowled at his shoes.

"Now, tell me," Mr. Erhard ordered. "Who opened the cage?"

"We don't know," Brian said. "We didn't."

"I put the lions in their cages myself and carefully locked them. None of our employees, not even Eric, would be stupid enough to unlock a cage and allow a dangerous animal to escape."

"Hey, I didn't do it," Eric said.

"You were here when I left."

"Just to do my job. It had to be one of those snoopy kids."

"Honest, we didn't touch the cage," Sean insisted. "The only reason we came here was because of Dan's note."

"What note?" Dan asked.

Brian held out the folded paper. Dan took it and read it. "I didn't write this," he said. "It's not even my handwriting."

Mr. Erhard grabbed the note and read it. Then Mr. Moroney took it. His voice shook as he said, "Boys, you must stay out of this area. It isn't safe."

Sean nodded. "I was afraid the lion was going to eat us."

"He probably wouldn't have eaten you, because he wasn't hungry," Dan said. "The lions were fed right after their performance. That's why Eric was here. Feeding the animals is part of his job."

Brian took a good look at Eric. He hadn't seemed either surprised or frightened when the lion was loose. And what had he told them? "Your snooping is going to get you in real trouble." Was trapping them with a lion Eric's idea of trouble?

Brian and Sean walked back to the main tent. Both of them had been so scared they still felt shaky.

"What happened with the lion was a warning to us," Brian said. "Someone was telling us to stay out of the case." He shook his head. "We didn't think. We got the note and ran off without stopping to figure things out."

"It's my fault," Sean said. "All I wanted to do was get away from Debbie Jean."

"Don't blame yourself, and don't blame Debbie Jean." Brian told him. "From now on we'll just be more careful and more sure of checking things out."

Sean looked up at Brian. "Then we're not going to give up?"

"No way," Brian said. "Dan's counting on us. This is a case we've got to solve."

When they returned to their seats, Sean was relieved to see that Debbie Jean had gone back to sit with her parents.

But she cupped her hands together and yelled down at Sean, "While you were gone, one of the clowns brought the monkey out. I got to shake his hand and you didn't."

Sean hunched his shoulders and pretended he didn't hear Debbie Jean. That didn't stop her. She yelled again, "The monkey jumped on a little bicycle and tried to escape, but the clown caught him, and you missed all the excitement! Ha, ha!"

Mrs. Quinn smiled at Sean. "Don't let Debbie Jean make you feel disappointed. There are even more exciting acts to come."

"Not too exciting, I hope," Sean said. His heart was just now beginning to settle down. "I've had about as much excitement as I can stand."

He leaned forward ready to watch the acts begin again, but Brian elbowed him in the ribs. "Don't count on it," he said. "Eric's over by the ropes, keeping an eye on us. For the rest of the evening I think we'd better stick close to Mom and Dad."

THE NEXT MORNING Brian and Sean
rode their bikes to the circus ground.
They found Dan in the lot picking up
soft-drink cans in one bag, trash in another.

"Let's go back to the costume tent," Brian
said. "There's something we've got to do."

They stopped, halfway across the lot. In the
distance they saw Crackers in full costume. As
they watched, the clown ran, stumbling into
the tent.

"Dad?" Dan cried. Dan, Brian, and Sean
ran after the clown.

But the costume tent was empty.

"Main tent!" Sean shouted. "He had to go in there!"

They stood just inside the entrance to the main tent, scanning the area. Without the bright lights it was dim and gloomy. A dusty, musty smell drifted from the sawdust-covered ground in the center ring.

Nothing moved, and no sound could be heard.

"That couldn't have been Dad," Dan said. "He was still asleep when I left the trailer, and that was only about fifteen minutes ago."

Brian and Sean followed Dan to the trailer he shared with his father. As they came in the door, Mr. Moroney turned from the small sink in the back of the trailer. He unplugged his electric razor and said, "Good morning, boys! You got an earlier start on the day than I did."

Brian glanced at the rumpled bed. "Mr.

Moroney, did you just get up?" he asked.

"Unfortunately," Mr. Moroney answered. "I'm usually up bright and early, but I didn't sleep well, what with one thing and another. I guess I was catching up on some shut-eye."

Sean glanced around. "Where's your costume?"

"Why, where it's supposed to be, in the costume tent."

"The costume!" Brian shouted. "We didn't check to see if it was there!"

"See you later, Dad," Dan said as he, Brian, and Sean rushed out of the trailer.

They made a dash to the costume tent. There was the clown costume on its hanger, the big shoes side by side underneath, and the wild yellow wig on its Styrofoam stand. Every part of the costume was just where it should be.

A car pulled up just outside, and they could

hear Sergeant Kerry's voice. "I'd like to speak to Marco Moroney," he told someone.

Brian, Sean, and Dan followed Sergeant Kerry as he was taken to the Moroney's trailer by one of the circus employees.

As Mr. Moroney came to the door and glanced down at Sergeant Kerry, his smile changed into a worried frown. "What can I do for you, Sergeant?" he asked.

"I'd like to talk to you about your whereabouts this morning," Sergeant Kerry said.

"I was right here," Mr. Moroney told him.

"During the last half hour."

Mr. Moroney looked puzzled. He walked down the steps of the trailer and stood before Sergeant Kerry. "I told you. I was here, asleep. I just got up a few minutes ago."

"That's right," Dan said.

Sergeant Kerry ignored Dan. He said to Mr.

Moroney, "Crackers the Clown was seen half an hour ago in a large drugstore out on the highway. One of those chain stores that's open twenty-four hours a day. After Crackers left, the clerks noticed that some display watches on the counter were missing."

"That wasn't Dad!" Dan insisted.

Brian stepped forward. "We were with Mr. Moroney just a few minutes ago. He had just finished shaving."

"Then you didn't actually see him in bed, asleep."

"Well, no," Brian said.

"We did see Crackers, though!" Sean burst out. "We saw the clown run into the costume tent. We went after him, but when we got there the tent was empty. So we went to find Mr. Moroney, and just like Bri told you, Mr. Moroney had just got out of bed and was shaving."

"What time was it when you saw the clown?" Sergeant Kerry asked Sean.

"I don't know," Sean said. "Ten or fifteen minutes ago?"

Brian looked embarrassed. "I didn't look at my watch."

"How about half an hour ago?" Sergeant Kerry asked. "Did you see Mr. Moroney at that time?"

Brian and Sean reluctantly shook their heads.

Mr. Moroney opened the door to his trailer. "Officer, I'd like you to come in and look around. You won't find those watches here, because I didn't take them. I've never set foot inside that drugstore you mentioned."

He walked into his trailer, leaving the door open wide. Sergeant Kerry took a step forward, but Brian grabbed his arm. "Someone is dressing in that clown costume and trying to make Mr. Moroney look guilty," he said. "Witnesses have seen a clown, but they haven't seen Mr. Moroney inside the costume. Everything you've got against Mr. Moroney is nothing more than circumstantial evidence."

"That's right," Kerry said. "But when we find the stolen property . . ."

Brian interrupted. "Before you do, I'm sure that Sean and I can figure out who the real thief is."

Sergeant Kerry shook his head. "I'm afraid this time you boys are wrong. However, whatever you have in mind—well, at least you can give it a try."

Brian pulled out his notebook and sat down on the ground. He motioned to Sean and Dan to join him. "We've got something we can figure out right now that might help us rule out some of our suspects," Brian said. "Which ones can fit into the Crackers costume?"

Dan, who'd been looking scared and miserable ever since Sergeant Kerry had arrived, sat up straight. "Way to go!" he said.

"Dale Erhard wouldn't be able to get into the costume," Sean said. "He's at least six inches taller than Mr. Moroney, and a lot heavier."

"Ray Spangler isn't heavier, but he's a good head taller than Dad," Dan said. "I don't see how he'd fit either."

Brian looked up from his notes. "Gus Hart is overweight, but the costume is baggy. He might be able to squeeze into it."

Sean thought a moment. "The way I remember it, the costume kind of hung on the clown. It wouldn't do that if it was stretched out over a fat stomach."

"Good point," Brian said. He crossed out

Gus Hart's name, too.

"That leaves us with Eric Lewis," Sean said.

Brian nodded. "He was arrested for shoplifting, he was there when the lion got loose, he threatened us, and he could fit inside Crackers's costume."

"Is that it?" Dan asked. "Do we tell the police to arrest Eric?"

"It's not that simple," Brian said. "We only have suspicions, not proof. We have to collect evidence and build a case."

"What does that mean?"

"It means that our next step is to find out exactly where every one of our suspects was when the first thefts took place. We have the exact time—4:02 P.M."

"Who should we start with?" Sean asked.

"Our number one suspect, Eric Lewis," Brian said.

None of them got to their feet. They looked at each other, and Sean could tell they were all thinking the same thing. Was it safe to question Eric? He was an awfully scary guy!

ERIC LEWIS SNARLED as Brian asked, "Where were you Thursday afternoon at four o'clock?"

"None of your business," Eric answered.

Dan tried to prompt him. "You were helping to put up the tents, weren't you?"

"Everybody knows that," Eric said. "Go away."

He leaned toward Brian and scowled.

Brian wished he were anyplace else, yet he didn't back down. "We want to prove that Marco Moroney didn't steal from the stores in Redoaks," he said. "We need you to help us."

Eric's laugh was bitter. "How am I supposed to help? By confessing to a crime I didn't commit? You kids go home and play baseball. Stop snooping around here."

Brian didn't move. "You didn't answer my question about what you were doing," he said.

"What was I doing?" Eric snapped out the words. "For your information, I was working hard, as I always do, and I don't like your suspicions. I told you to stop snooping around here or you'd be sorry. You didn't pay attention the first time, but you'd better listen to me now!"

Eric stomped off before Brian could say another word.

"I think he did it," Sean whispered.

"Remember, a good investigator keeps an open mind," Brian said. "Let's talk to Ray Spangler."

They found Mr. Spangler sunning himself in a canvas folding chair outside the Spanglers' trailer. He brought down his feet from the small folding table on which they'd been propped and smiled. "What can I do for you boys?" he asked.

"Just answer a question," Brian said.

Mr. Spangler laughed. "Like 'Where were you the night of the murder?'"

"You got it," Brian said. "Only change it to: 'Where were you at four o'clock, Thursday afternoon?'"

"That's an easy answer," Mr. Spangler said. "Laura Lee was napping inside our trailer, and I was playing cards right here in this very spot with Pinkie Jones. Pinkie's the elephant trainer. Pinkie and I finished our game around four-fifteen, and he left. Laura woke up around four-thirty, and we went for a drive. We like to get a look at some of the towns we visit." He smiled. "Redoaks is a nice little place. I bet you like living here."

"Yeah, we do," Sean began, but Brian held up a hand.

"Let's get back to your answer, Mr. Spangler. If we ask Pinkie Jones where he was, will his story be the same as yours?"

"Absolutely," Mr. Spangler said.

"Then Pinkie's your alibi," Sean said.

Mr. Spangler's friendly attitude quickly disappeared. "I don't need an alibi. I didn't commit the crime," he said.

Dan led Brian and Sean to Pinkie Jones. Pinkie told them that on Thursday afternoon he'd been playing cards with Ray Spangler while Laura Lee was sleeping. "Did you see Laura Lee?" Brian asked. "Do you know for sure she was in the trailer?"

"Nope. I left before she woke up."

"Do you remember what time you were with Mr. Spangler?"

Mr. Jones shook his head. "I haven't worn a watch for years," he said. "Don't need one. Spangler said it was four-fifteen, and he thought he'd wake up Laura Lee so they could go for a drive."

"That means you can't really be sure of the time," Brian said. He made another note.

"Why'd I need to look at a watch when somebody had just told me the time?" Mr. Jones asked. He spread out his arms. "Look, that's all I know. There's nothing more I can tell you."

"Thanks," Brian said. As soon as Mr. Jones was out of hearing range, he glanced at his notes. "Sergeant Kerry said that Gus Hart claimed he was at home, going over his expenses. He'd left his store in the hands of his manager."

"Why is Mr. Hart still a suspect?" Sean asked.

"Take a look back by the animals' cages," Brian said.

Sean turned to see what Brian meant. There was Mr. Hart, poking with a cane inside and around the bales of hay that were stacked and ready for use.

"What's he doing?" Dan whispered.

"Why don't we ask him?" Brian said.

He, Sean, and Dan walked up behind Mr. Hart, who was so busy he hadn't noticed them. He jumped and yelped when Brian asked, "What are you looking for, Mr. Hart?"

Mr. Hart leaned against the hay. He put one hand on his chest and breathed deeply.

"Don't scare me like that!" he said.

"I'm sorry," Brian said. "I just asked what you're looking for."

"My property!" Mr. Hart said. "That clown hid it around here somewhere, I know. Once I find it, the police can arrest that clown, and put him in jail, and Redoaks will get rid of all these traveling shows."

Eric stepped out from behind the bales of hay. He glowered at Mr. Hart. "You don't belong here," he said. "Get off the property! Now!"

"I-I have a r-right to search for my stolen property!" Mr. Hart said.

Eric's lips twisted in a nasty smile. "Or maybe plant some jewelry that the police can find later."

Mr. Hart's face grew red, and he sputtered. "That's a crazy idea! I'd never! I—I—"

Eric shoved his face into Mr. Hart's. "Get out

of here!" he shouted.

Mr. Hart turned and ran.

"You, too," Eric said to Brian.

"In a minute," Brian said.

He motioned for Sean and Dan to follow him to the main tent where two workers were sweeping.

"Hi," Brian said. "Did any of you see Eric on Thursday afternoon at four o'clock?"

One of the men smiled. "Probably. Off and on."

The other man said, "Eric's not too dependable. Sometimes he's on hand, workin' up a sweat. Then sometimes you need him, and he's off behind a pile of tarps takin' a snooze."

"Then you can't say for sure Eric was here at the circus lot at four o'clock?" Brian asked.

"Nope," the first man said, "but ask around. You might find somebody who was workin' with him."

Brian began walking toward Dale Erhard's trailer. "Last on our list," he said to Sean and Dan.

As they approached the trailer, they could hear loud voices arguing.

"Why don't you listen to reason, Marco?" Mr. Erhard shouted angrily. "I keep telling you, we're losing so much money the circus is going to fail. Why let that happen and lose everything?"

"Maybe there's something we can still do," Mr. Moroney said. "More publicity? Bigger ads in the newspapers?"

"That won't work. If you're smart, you'll sell out to me. It will be a struggle, but, without the profits being divided in two, I think I can make a go of it."

"No!" Mr. Moroney thundered. "The circus

has been in my family for three generations. I'm not going to give it up!"

"That's stupid!"

"I don't care what you think! It's my decision!"

Mr. Moroney slammed open the trailer door. The boys ducked out of sight as he stomped toward his own trailer.

Brian led the way through the still-open door into Mr. Erhard's trailer and said, "Is it okay if we ask you a question?"

Mr. Erhard sighed. "One question. What is it?"

"Where were you at four o'clock on Thursday afternoon?" Brian asked.

Mr. Erhard had to think for a moment before he answered, "Right here. I was busy writing the weekly salary checks for the circus help."

"Did anyone see you here?"

"No one."

"Can anyone give you an alibi?"

"I made two phone calls during that time," Mr. Erhard said wearily. "But I imagine the police have already checked those out."

He frowned. "Look, kids, I'm tired. You said you'd ask one question, and I think you asked three. No more. That's it. Go home."

"Thanks for your help," Brian said

After they left the trailer, Dan groaned and said, "We didn't learn anything."

"Yes, we did," Sean said.

"What? That everybody was here? That nobody could have stolen the stuff except my dad?"

"Don't get discouraged," Sean told him. "Somebody was lying to us. All we have to do is figure out who."

"Oh, sure," Dan said. "Just how are you going to do that?"

Brian spoke up. "It won't be easy. I think we'll have to set up a stakeout."

9

BRIAN WENT ON. "Since the stolen items haven't been found yet, I don't think our fake Crackers clown is through."

"You mean there's going to be another burglary?" Sean asked.

"Yes," Brian answered. "But maybe this time when the police come to check out Mr. Moroney, they'll find some of the stuff that was stolen in Mr. Moroney's trailer."

Dan's eyes grew bigger. "Then everybody will be sure my dad committed the crimes! How are we going to stop the thief from framing Dad?"

"By finding out who the thief is," Brian said.

Dan sighed. "We haven't been able to find out yet."

"But now we'll set a trap and be ready," Sean said. "Won't we, Bri? You have a plan, I hope."

"Yes, I do," Brian said. He looked to each side. There were plenty of places where people could hide and overhear them. "Let's go someplace private," Brian said.

They walked to where the cars and their bikes were parked. Brian laid out his idea. "We'll ride off the circus lot, so everyone will think that we've gone. Then we'll sneak back and hide in the costume tent. We may be there a while, but if the thief decides to commit a crime before the afternoon circus show, he'll come and pick up the costume pretty soon."

Debbie Jean popped out from behind the nearest truck. "I'm ready," she said. "I love hiding and jumping out at people."

"Debbie Jean!" Sean said. "You don't belong here!"

"Yes, I do," she said. "I told you I was going to help you."

"You have no business following us!" Sean shouted.

"I wasn't following you. I was parking my bike between those trucks when you came over here. It's not my fault you didn't see me." She smiled at Dan. "If someone's trying to frame your father, then I want to help catch him."

Dan smiled back. Sean felt like barfing.

"Okay," Brian said. "Stick with us." In a low voice he said to Sean, "It'll be easier than trying to get rid of her."

They all hopped on their bikes and rode off the lot. They stashed their bikes under some bushes around the corner and went back to the tents through the route customers would take when they came to the two o'clock show. Silently, hoping they hadn't been seen, they slipped into the costume tent.

Debbie Jean stopped so suddenly that Sean nearly ran into her. "Ooooh!" she squealed. "Look at all the feathers and sequins and spangles! Cool!"

Dan glanced around the room. "I'll hide behind the dressing tables. Sean, why don't you squeeze behind the rack of costumes?"

"Look! Look at me! I'm gorgeous!" Debbie Jean wobbled toward them in a pair of pink satin shoes trimmed with glittering beads and sequins.

"Take those off!" Sean ordered. "They're not yours. Besides, they're way too big for you. You're tripping and stumbling all over the place."

"Sean's right," Dan said. "Maria, one of the bareback riders wears those in the parade. She'd be real mad if she caught you wearing them."

"Oh, all right." Debbie Jean put the shoes back where she found them and put on her own sneakers.

Brian smiled. "I just thought of something important," he said. "When we were talking about who . . ."

Sean let out a yell, interrupting Brian. "Crackers's costume's gone!" he said. "The thief has already been here!"

"Oh no!" Dan said.

"Don't blame me. You're always blaming

me," Debbie Jean said to Sean.

"Everybody chill," Brian said. "We missed the thief before he left to commit his crime, but it doesn't matter. We'll catch him when he gets back."

"How?" Sean asked. "Last time we chased him, and he ran into the main tent and disappeared."

"Is the thief a magician?" Debbie Jean asked.

Brian shook his head, but he smiled. "It's not going to take magic to solve this case. A few minutes ago I realized that there was one big clue we missed . . . up till now, that is. I think I just figured out who the thief is."

"Who?" Sean asked.

"Who?" Dan asked at the same time.

"Tell me. I won't tell anyone else," Debbie Jean said.

"Let's work out a few things first," Brian said.

"I want to be sure I'm right before I say any-thing."

He pointed to a large costume trunk in one corner of the tent. "Debbie Jean, you said you like to hide and jump out at people. Well now's your chance. You hide behind that trunk and keep your eyes open. When the clown comes in, jump out and yell."

"Yell what?" Debbie Jean asked.

"Anything. I don't care. Yell, 'Gotcha!' if you want. Sean, you hide in back of the dressing table closest to the tent flap. When the clown— and anybody with the clown—runs into the main tent, you run out the other way. Yell to the circus workers for help, and call the police."

Sean's eyes grew wide, but he immediately scrunched down behind the dressing table. Debbie Jean climbed behind the trunk.

Brian motioned to Dan to follow him into

the main tent. "Do you know how to work the spotlights?" Brian asked.

"Sure," Dan said.

"Can you send lots of light anywhere we want?"

"You bet."

"Okay," Brian said. "Get the lights ready to be switched on and wait."

"Where are you going to be?"

"I'll be right next to you," Brian told him.

They climbed up to one of the platforms that held the spotlights.

As they settled down to wait, Dan whispered, "When is all this going to happen?"

Brian looked at his watch. "Very soon," he said.

Within less than two minutes they heard Debbie Jean give a bloodcurdling scream, then yell, "Freeze! This is the SWAT team! You're surrounded!"

"She probably watches a lot of TV," Dan said.

The flap to the costume tent burst open, and in the dim light Brian could see two figures dash into the main tent. The tall one was faster than the short one, who stumbled and staggered while trying to run.

The tall figure leaped upward, then disappeared into the darkness. The short figure followed.

Brian jumped up and shouted, "Lights! To the top of the tent!"

Dan hit the switches, and a wide beam shot upward to the platform where Ray and Laura Lee Spangler perched, clinging to the ropes. Laura Lee had pulled off the large, heavy clown shoes, but she still wore the rest of the costume, and her face was heavily painted in clown makeup.

A number of the circus hands ran into the tent. Brian saw Pinkie Jones, Marco Moroney, and Eric Lewis among them.

Sean ran in shouting, "Sergeant Kerry's on his way!"

Debbie Jean jumped right into the middle of the onlookers, yelling, "We caught them! We caught them!"

As the crowd grew larger, everyone stared upward at the Spanglers, trapped in the spotlight's beam. Brian shouted, "There's the fake Crackers and his accomplice. Keep them up there until the police get here."

Minutes later, Sergeant Kerry arrived and ordered the Spanglers to come down. He listened to the evidence the Casebusters had gathered, then made the arrest and read the Spanglers their rights.

"We were told that Marco wouldn't go to jail," Laura Lee told Sergeant Kerry. "What we did was only supposed to get him to sell his share of the circus."

"Be quiet, Laura Lee," Ray Spangler said.

"Framing an innocent man for a crime isn't a prank," Sergeant Kerry told her. "Both of you, come with me. We'll get your statements down at headquarters."

"Sergeant Kerry, wait a minute, please," Brian said. He looked at Laura Lee. "You said that somebody told you that Marco Moroney wouldn't go to jail. Who was it?"

"You don't have to tell them anything, Laura Lee," Ray said.

Laura Lee's eyes were wide, and she shivered. "I'm not going to take all the blame," she said.

"Dale Erhard told me."

"Did Dale Erhard plan this, or did you and your husband?" Sergeant Kerry asked.

"Don't blame Ray!" Laura Lee cried. "Dale planned the whole thing!"

Sean shook his head. "Why'd you go along with a dumb plan like that?" he asked.

"Yeah, why?" Debbie Jean echoed.

Laura Lee began to cry. "Because Dale promised that if we did what he said, he'd tear up our contract, and we could accept the offer from the French circus."

"We'll talk about all this downtown," Sergeant Kerry said. "In the meantime we'll pick up Erhard."

One of the circus hands spoke up. "Dale took off in the brown sedan," he said.

Eric's smile twisted into a sneer. "He won't go far," he said. "I was supposed to get the gas tank filled up, and I forgot."

The circus people drifted out of the tent, but Mr. Moroney ran up to shake Brian's and Sean's hands. "Thank you, boys! Thank you!" he cried. "You're great private investigators!"

"Yeah!" Dan said. "Brian, you knew Laura Lee was the clown. How did you figure it out?"

"We thought about who could fit into Crackers the Clown's outfit, but we didn't think about the shoes. The shoes were way too big for Laura Lee. She could hardly walk in them, so she kept stumbling. Those stumbles were too real to be a part of anybody's act. Then, when we were in the costume tent . . ."

Sean began laughing. "I know! You saw Debbie Jean wobbling around like a sick gooney bird in those high-heeled shoes, and that made you think about Laura Lee stumbling around!"

"I did not look like a sick gooney bird!" Debbie Jean snapped. "I looked gorgeous."

"Sick gooney birds think they look gorgeous, too." Sean said. He laughed so hard he bent over, holding his stomach.

Mr. Moroney shook Debbie Jean's hand, too. "Thank you for your help in solving the case," he said.

"You guys were great," Dan said, and the worried look came back to his face. "But Dad's problems aren't over."

"Sure, they are," Brian said. "Mr. Erhard kept the books and probably most of the money. You said your performances drew big crowds, so there had to be a lot of money involved. The police—maybe even the Feds—will find out how much and where it went."

Dan smiled. "That wasn't exactly what I meant," he said. "I figured the money will show up. I was thinking that Dad could take over the job as the ringmaster and lion tamer, but where is he going to find another pair of trapeze artists?"

"Don't look at us," Sean said, and laughed again. "Brian would look awful in tights."

JOAN LOWERY NIXON is a renowned writer of children's mysteries. She is the author of more than eighty books and the only four-time recipient of the prestigious Edgar Allan Poe Award for the best juvenile mystery of the year.

☾

"*I was asked by* Disney Adventures *magazine if I could write a short mystery. I decided to write about two young boys who help their father, a private investigator, solve crimes. These boys, Brian and Sean, are actually based on my grandchildren, who are the same ages as the characters. My first Casebusters story was a piece about a ghost that haunts an inn. This derives from a legendary Louisiana inn I visited which was allegedly haunted. Later, I learned the owner had made up the entire tale, and I used that angle in the story.*"

— JOAN LOWERY NIXON